SHE REX

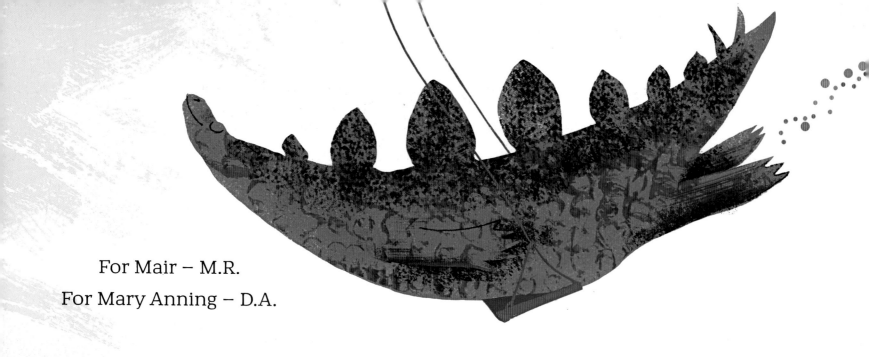

For Mair – M.R.

For Mary Anning – D.A.

BLOOMSBURY CHILDREN'S BOOKS
Bloomsbury Publishing Plc
50 Bedford Square, London WC1B 3DP, UK

BLOOMSBURY, BLOOMSBURY CHILDREN'S BOOKS and the Diana logo
are trademarks of Bloomsbury Publishing Plc

First published in Great Britain in 2020 by Bloomsbury Publishing Plc

A catalogue record for this book is available
from the British Library

ISBN 978 1 4088 7610 7 (HB)
ISBN 978 1 4088 7608 4 (PB)
ISBN 978 1 4088 7609 1 (eBook)

2 4 6 8 10 9 7 5 3 1

Printed and bound in China by Leo Paper Products, Heshan, Guangdong

All papers used by Bloomsbury Publishing Plc are natural,
recyclable products from wood grown in well-managed forests.
The manufacturing processes conform
to the environmental regulations of the country of origin

To find out more about our authors and books visit www.bloomsbury.com
and sign up for our newsletters

SHE REX

Michelle Robinson

Illustrated by
Deborah Allwright

BLOOMSBURY
CHILDREN'S BOOKS
LONDON OXFORD NEW YORK NEW DELHI SYDNEY

Ed won't let me share his toys.
He says, "Dinos are for boys."

But I don't need them.
Move it, mister . . .

meet T. Rex's bigger sister . . .

She Rex is a big and burly,
multicoloured dino girly.

I just saw one.
I should know . . .

"Well, if you saw one.
Where'd it go?"

She went out hunting, probably.

My brother laughs out loud at me.
"You **seriously** think you saw
a multicoloured dinosaur?
Big fat NOTHING'S what you've seen.
I know best. T. Rex was **green**."

You're right. Some parts were green, I think.
Plus purple, yellow, blue and pink!
"Pink dinosaurs?" Ed snorts. "How lame!

I've had enough of your daft game.
Girlosaurs? Yuck! Count me out.
They'd sing and skip and prance about!"

He carries on, "They'd wear high heels,
invite their friends around for meals.
They'd skip through meadows holding hands
in flowery dresses like our Gran's!
I bet you think their scales were frilly."

"Ed," I say, "you're being silly!"

My dinosaurs are mean, for sure.

And boy, oh boy, can these girls . . .

ROAR!

They're just as fierce as any boys.

"Come on, girls, let's make some noise!"

Girlosaurs are big and strong.

But Ed says, "Maisy, you are wrong.
You haven't seen one, I should know –
the dinos died out YEARS ago!"

Dying out? No, not these ones –
they're DINING out on chips and buns.

Ed folds his arms. He huffs. He sighs.
He shakes his head. He rolls his eyes.
"I'm the expert. I know best.
There's NO She Rex
and you're a pest."

I stomp my foot.
I've had **enough**.
She Rex **is** real –
and really **tough**!

"Oh, yeah?" Ed says.
"Well how d'you know?"

I say, "She's right behind you . . ."

"WOAH!"

Behold! She Rex!
The lizard queen!

The **fiercest** girl
there's ever been!
Her **giant feet.**
Her **massive teeth.**

Her rumbling
belly underneath!

She **hunts!** She **eats!** She **roars!** She **fights!**

Girl dinosaurs have equal bites.

Plus I **told** you they weren't dead.

Admit it, I'm the **expert** . . .

"Ed?"

"Okay," Ed says. "You saw **She Rex.**
Perhaps we could play **pirates** next?"

"Fine," I say. "I GUESS I'll play . . ."

"But Blackbeard is a GIRL – okay?"